Names of the Dead

Tristan Gray

Copyright © 2020 Tristan Gray

All rights reserved.

ISBN: d979-8-8571627-4-3

ACKNOWLEDGMENTS

It's been a weird year and having a place and person to call home has made a real difference to feeling the security I've needed to create. My partner Jude has been that for me, and I can never thank her enough for being here.

To my family, who continue to be a constant inspiration and encouragement even whilst we're trapped hundreds of miles away from one another.

Thank again to Gillian Hamnett from Dark Sky Pages for her vital help with the Scots language spoken by Annis. Ensuring a tale drawing from our real-world languages is true and loyal is a vital part of bringing a culture to the page and without her expertise it could never have happened.

Thank you to Margaret Kingsbury, editor for Salt & Sage Books, for her work on the developmental edit that helped shape the story and stitch together the plot holes and strained metaphors that plagued the earlier editions of the script.

Thanks to Matthew King who took on the task of proof-reading the text and putting in some final changes before publication. I'm terrible for rushing things through and leaving odds and ends spare so this really is a manuscript-saving step!

NAMES OF THE DEAD

The sea was still as glass beneath the ship as it drifted into harbour. The port of Ghav Rhien loomed over them, the stone walls and towers of its fortified heart protruding from the cliffs above. It was both a statement and a memorial to the one hundred sieges over the centuries. No one had come to the isle with drawn swords and left it with both their blade and pride intact.

The soft swell of the water lapped against the pebbled shore and the scent of salt and seaweed filled the air. This was a place of rest for many a traveller, and a home to many more whose travels had ended.

Fiadh's eyes cast over the bay with a warmth she felt deep in her chest. There was something about home, with the meeting of the granite and the sea, and it had been many a season she had sailed past Ghav Rhien and looked to it with yearning. Today, finally, she had been given a good reason to make landing here.

There was someone waiting on that harbour for her. Old men in white robes and the symbols of faith didn't tend to watch over docks in the middle of the afternoon at a whim. He stood as he always had, hands clasped before him, below the embossed bronze ornaments that hung about his neck and glittered in the sun.

As they drifted in against the jetty, Fiadh stepped onto the woodwork before the boat came to a halt, dropping ashore with her sack and scabbard over one shoulder, a skip and a smile to the grim features of her one-man welcoming party.

"Brianan! It has been too long!" she said, arms wide in welcome.

Brianan did not share her enthusiasm.

"Fare you well, Crow?" Though his words were warm his tone was cold; his arms remained wrapped in his robes. This was a frostiness she'd encountered before – the chill of someone whose mind was occupied with the misfortune of others.

More than just his grim features set her on edge. There was something else here, a sound that rang just at the edge of her hearing, beyond what she could grasp or accurately describe. An eerie keening that drifted and hung over the water.

"I…" she hesitated, trying to shake the sound from her head. "I fare well enough, old man, my bones aren't quite aged enough to bother me when the storms roll in." His eyebrow rose at her words, though the scepticism was at least a marked improvement on no expression at all.

His look was made no friendlier by the cruel upturn in his lip cast by a scar that ran from his chin to a milky-white eye and his temple. A legacy of an age where the druid had wielded more than books and tales of old gods.

"Your face may not bear the lines of age, Fiadh, but you have changed. I can see the weight of a lifetime in your eyes. I fear there are some things we were never meant to see. You, like Eònan, may have seen too much for so few journeys around the wheel."

She scoffed at his melodramatic tone. He'd learnt to intone his words with the weight and cadence of a millennia, even if he were only discussing what food graced his plate. Such habits learned from the filidhean bards doesn't slip easily.

"I travel all the way here," Fiadh said, skipping ahead and turning to continue whilst walking backwards up towards the town beyond. "Risking my very life to these treacherous seas at your beckoning and you greet me with jibes at my age. Dear Brianan, you spoil me so!"

Brianan's mood remained cold as the deepest winter. "I assure you, Fiadh, I would not have made such a request lightly. The clouds hang low over Ghav Rhien and I fear my ability to lead it to the right path is swiftly waning. It is my hope that you may breach those clouds and bring some light back to this place."

He had continued to speak even as Fiadh turned away and flipped a coin into the waiting hands of a merchant in exchange for a glazed bread, continuing to walk in expectant silence as she fell in step with him and mumbled her delight around the sweet treat.

"So," she managed around another bite. "Doom and darkness, driving out ancient evils and restoring us to the natural order of things. What kind of curse has fallen under your watch, old man?"

The route around them began to wind as they left the harbour market and made their way past the scattered homes thrown up against the hillside that dominated the isle.

"I would not have called on you for a simple matter, you know this." The druid was a smaller figure than she remembered. The years had drained away much of his stature and the slump of his shoulders belied the familiar determination of his eyes. "I am not so old that I cannot handle such matters myself."

"I apologise for wounding your pride so," Fiadh said. The keening of the docks was drawing closer now, and though those around her could not hear it as she could, she saw that it had drawn a shadow over the people of the hill. As the wail drifted over them, eyes cast fearfully to the fortress above, shutters brought closed even against the sunlight and still winds.

This was not the way people responded to sudden frights coming in the night, but rather that of a community held under the foreboding air of a threat held over them for seasons.

"He cannot sleep, the Rìgh, he is plagued by shadows that come to him in the night and speak to him alone. He wakes with fits of anguish, preoccupied by the past at the expense of the present." The druid's own eyes were cast up and past her to the walls as he spoke.

"Eònan has long since ceased listening to my council, after my failures to guide him from his dark thoughts with what little help I could offer. There is another here, now, who has his ear. I fear his counsel is guiding him down a misjudged path and into the arms of those who wish him no good fortune."

Fiadh followed his gaze to see helms glinting on the battlements, mismatched spear tips and shields gathered in watch over the path.

"Those are not Daoine," she said.

"They are not," Brianan replied. "The Rìgh in the depths of his darkness has cast suspicions on all those who once stood at his side. I am one of the few who remain. The Àrdish and Sjøfolk now man his keep and drain his coffers, the very people he sacrificed so much to defend this rock from."

"Yet you have remained?" Fiadh asked.

"I fear not for many more days. This is my final cast of the dice. You are who I have turned to in my last moments on this isle and my last under the eye of Eònan. I will not leave here regretting that I did not do all I could to save my liege from his torments."

He was a grim and sour individual, but Fiadh had always respected the fierce loyalty and honour that Brianan held close to his heart. There were few she knew would fight harder for their duty, even to those who had long ceased to deserve it.

"Some people are doomed to linger on their past mistakes. I will not be one of them, Fiadh. We cannot change what we have done. We may only come to terms with it and let it change us," said Brianan.

"And what if we cannot save him, what then?" she asked.

"What's done is done," he said, the words intoned with all the authority of a man who had said them many times to audiences of the faithful.

The doors to the fortress loomed over them as they reached the crest of the hill, great slabs of wood shipped from oaks far away piled upon one another in the form of a gate. Two men bedecked in mail and capped helms stood on either side of the opening and nodded to the druid in recognition, letting the pair past and into the courtyard beyond.

Quite unlike the bustle Fiadh remembered, the clearing within the walls was practically empty. Further guards were scattered here and there, glancing suspiciously in their direction but just as frequently over their shoulders as if their shadows crept up upon them.

The hall of the Rìgh sat cupped in the shadow of a cliff that hung over the fortress: a squat complex built generations ago by the first lords who seized control of the waters around the isle, its many timbers cracked by the waters of a hundred storms and decorated with trails of moss and vines. Above its door a carved mural displayed the battles of Eònan's ancestors against men, serpents, and great monsters of the deeps.

Now their successor had shut himself away in fear from shadows and cries in the night.

Like the gate before, the guards at the hall's door nodded to Brianan and drew back the bar that held the door shut. It may be his final cast of the dice, but the druid still clearly claimed the respect of those who remained at the Rìgh's side. With a nod in return, Fiadh followed Brianan into the torch-lit interior.

The hall within dwarfed the other structures of the isle, the staunch pillars legacies of the centuries it had stood here. Over time the complex had spread from this meeting place, connected to it by a half-dozen corridors radiating outwards from it. In the silence within Rìgh Eònan sat slumped in a throne of ornate woodwork, yet more carvings of the monsters and heroes of Ghav Rhien's past looming over him, locked in eternal combat. He had aged in the years since Fiadh had seen him last, the proud brows and chin now wreathed in scraggly white hairs. Beneath his iron circlet his hair fell long across his shoulders in thin wisps.

The men standing about his seat were not the old champions who had stood at his side for a hundred minor skirmishes over the isles. Gone were the trusted advisors of his forefathers and the famed warriors who carried their names. Instead there was a scattering of young men and women of every possible people and garb, a collection so disparate they could have been collected by hands grasping at random from across the known world. They stood in silence, their eyes darting nervously between their lord and their new guests.

All the better to ensure they could have no possible loyalties nor affections here that came before the Rìgh.

There was one among them, however, who set Fiadh's hairs on end. At the left arm of Eònan stood a gangly figure so overwhelmed in their grey robes that they might as well have been hung from a rack. Beneath their cowl was a mask in white marble, and a string of bells lay across their shoulders to waist.

From their neck hung the symbol of Alwealda, spun to appear in the form of a two-headed key. The priest's mask faced them; eyes hidden behind the expressionless visage.

Here, standing before the silent gathering, Fiadh could hear the keening she had heard below more clearly: a high wail carried through these halls, an otherworldly cry beyond the hearing of the scattering of men and women gathered, but nevertheless she could see its presence set them on edge.

The wail wasn't voiceless, then. There were names in the air, drifting in and out, wrapping themselves like spectral hands about the shoulders of those gathered here. She could see the men around the Rìgh standing uneasily, shuffling their feet, glancing towards one another and into the corners at nothing, rubbing at sleep-deprived eyes.

Over them all the wail continued, carrying names along with it. Caoimhe, Domhnall, Rhona, Fionn. They repeated in that order, always the same, always drifting just at the edge of the wail that she alone in this hall could pick from the air.

"Come," came Eònan's croaked acknowledgement, a hand raised in an exhausted wave in their direction. In concert Fiadh and Brianan bowed their heads and walked forward, their footsteps echoing in a silence only broken by the uncomfortable shifting of the guard.

When they were halfway to the throne, Fiadh took the druid's lead to kneel before the withered remnants of the warrior sat upon it. It had been too long since she had last seen him, too long for him to recognise the face of the girl she had been last they had crossed paths in the town below.

"It has been some time since you last came to my hall, Brianan, old friend. You once stood at my side, yet now instead you spread rumours and messages far afield to tell the tales of my woes." Eònan's rasp grew harsher the longer he spoke, though if Brianan was stung by those words he showed no sign of it.

"Yes, I know what you have been doing. I have heard of your missives and calls for aid to complete the work of protecting me from the darkness that has seized my domain. The work you failed to do you now turn to others to complete in your place."

Fiadh desperately wanted to see how the servant of Alwealda was responding to this tirade but stayed bowed alongside Brianan in silence. Now was likely not the ideal time to let curiosities breach whatever stillness they had found in the midst of Eònan's paranoia.

Brianan remained strong as he replied, "I return with Fiadh, of Tur Eumor. She might yet be able to find the source of your dark dreams, I thought…"

"A Crow? You bring me a Crow, old man, as your final bid to redeem yourself in my eyes?" Eònan cut off the druid with further weak waves of his hand before he continued his thoughts. "After you failed to drive out the keening of the dead from my halls?"

"A Crow!" Eònan laughed, but there was no mirth in his rasped cackling, the sound was grim and cruel. "After all this time, it is you who would bring a servant of the Ríagan to the doors of my very chambers."

Fiadh knew that tone, the tone of someone who felt powerless finally seizing on something they could wield control over, something they could hold over someone else and feel strong again. There were few more dangerous things on this earth.

"You've led me to my death, druid," Fiadh hissed under her breath.

"I have faith," he whispered in reply. "You didn't become the last of your order without some skill avoiding the hangman and the stake, Crow."

Fiadh cursed and she cast her gaze back to the baleful eyes of Eònan glaring down at her. "I'm the last Crow because the rest of them had friends like you."

"I made a deal, Brianan," the Rìgh continued. "A deal to make sure the Crows never again set foot on my isle and meddled in affairs they had no right to be sticking their long beaks into."

He pulled himself to his feet, shaking hands clinging to its arms and teeth gritting against the effort, but his eyes never left the pair kneeling before him.

"I didn't watch the Tur burn just to have my advisors welcome them into my halls and plague my very shadow."

Fiadh flinched at that. He had been there? Rìgh Eònan had been there when Tur Eumor fell, the destruction of her home and sanctuary?

Her teeth ground together as she bit back the fury and hurt, the pain bringing tears to her eyes. All this time, all these years searching for the bastards who had come across the sea and brought ruin on the Tur, leaving her a wanderer. Brianan had been serving one of them this entire time.

Head still bowed, she could see the priest of Alwealda lean in and begin to whisper to the Rìgh. She could see it clearly now, the darkness that hung over the lord, the dark rings beneath his eyes, the weakness that left his back arched even when stood, the eyes filled with suspicion and anger. This wasn't the strong ruler who had secured the isle from innumerable foes by the point of a spear in years past. This was a man gripped and ruled by his own fear.

As the priest whispered their reply from behind that etched marble mask, Eònan's withered gaze fell upon her and their eyes met, albeit briefly. Beneath the veil of hate she could see the desperation of a man surrounded by strangers who could not aid him against whatever spirit haunted this hall. A man who in his darkest hour had driven away those who had failed him, only to turn to those who would weave whatever remained of his hope for their own ends.

Perhaps, all those years ago, those very same whispers had brought him to the Tur and upended her own life into the dark and chaotic seas.

Eònan snarled and tore his gaze away, feebly waving off his devout advisor. "Take them away, give them lodging elsewhere. I no longer wish to see either of them in my hall. I wish to think; all this clamour clouds my thoughts. I must think."

The Rìgh's face twisted and twitched as his eyes searched the hall, over the heads of those gathered before him.

"Enough! None will question my judgement, I will have silence!" he snapped, those about him starting at the sudden command. No one present had spoken.

But Fiadh could hear them, just as the Rìgh now could. Those names continued to drift across the hall, the keening falling in and out, jumbled in the midst of indecipherable mutterings and whispers.

Eònan gripped his throne hard in one hand and the other cast about in the air like he sought to free it of thoughts not his own. "Away, away, I must think, I must have silence. All of you, away!"

Brianan nudged her arm and stood. She joined him and they backed away from the throne even as other servants began to filter out of the hall through the corridors leading them deeper into the complex. This was clearly far from the first time they had been instructed to depart with such abrupt and unprompted vagaries. Few remained where they stood, the priest of Alwealda and a handful of his mercenary champions among them.

Fiadh grabbed Brianan's arm roughly the moment they had moved down a passage and out of sight of the throne. His eyes went wide at the harshness of her grip.

"Who are they, Brianan?" she snapped in as low a tone as she could muster.

"Please, Fiadh, I didn't know, none of us did!" Brianan stammered, before realising he was answering a question that had not been asked. "Wait, who are who?" the druid finally replied, eyes glancing back from where they had come, half expecting more ears to be leaning into his words.

"The names drifting on the wind. They portend the dead, the cry of a caoineag grips this place. Something has trapped it here."

The druid nodded understanding to that. "Who is portended to die?" he asked. "Is it Eònan? Townspeople?"

"The names, Caoimhe, Domhnall, Rhona…"

"Shhhh!" Brianan cut her off suddenly, finger raised. "Never speak those names again here, Crow, lest you be left to hang from the ramparts before the night's end."

Fiadh roughly brushed his finger away. "You and I both know that unless I can lift this curse that fate is what is intended for me. Who are they?"

"It makes no sense. Those can't be the names you heard."

"Why not?" she snapped.

"They're dead." his eyes locked with hers, reinforcing the earnestness of his words. "Have been for years. Since before you even washed up on these shores and into my life. They're the Rìgh's family, killed when Jarl Vestamr seized the islands. That first name you spoke, that was his sister."

"Why can't their names be spoken?" Her grip drew him further from the hall as their heads leant in towards one another, keeping their whispers safe from the servants still making their way from the throne.

"He never truly recovered from their loss," Brianan

said. "He was a bright young man in his youth, always first to look to the horizon and ask how far his ship could take him. Their deaths changed him, casting a great melancholy over him. He may bend the knee to Vestamr, but he never truly forgave him; those deaths have hung between them ever since and will follow them until one or both are sent to their graves."

Footsteps began to sound from the hall behind them, cutting short Fiadh's questions.

"Are you sure they were killed? They cannot have survived?" she said.

"Sure as I am that I stand before you, Fiadh. I saw them laid to rest, I assisted the master who carried out the burials, learned from the song of the filidh who sung their tale. They are as dead as the rock we stand upon."

It wasn't possible. A caoineag haunted the nights of places where the ends of those dear to inhabitants were due. Their cry could bring the chill of death upon a household, preparing them for the loss that was to come.

But never would their wails come beneath the risen sun, nor continue for months on end, nor would the names on their tongues be those of the already dead.

If Eònan did not have her killed by the morn it was possible this caoineag would, disturbed in the midst of its powerful grip over this hall. For the first time in years Fiadh felt the faint stirring of panic rising in her chest.

It was broken by the arrival of one of Eònan's party of mercenaries and two servants. Brianan nodded his acknowledgement to them and departed down the hallway, abandoning her to this new heavily armed company. This warrior was one of the slighter one of their number, but his armament was that of an experienced fighter and the crisscross of scars across his arms betrayed a storied career before arriving in this forsaken place.

"Please, the Rìgh has insisted you be treated as our guest and stay till the morn, you may leave with the tide. We will show you to your chambers," one of the servants spoke, gesturing further down the hallway. So it began, she thought.

As they joined her, Fiadh's ears pricked as the mercenary muttered to himself. It wasn't quite loud enough for her to catch the words but the tongue was unmistakable. He wasn't speaking in Cànan, the language she shared with the people of this isle, but in Àrdish, clearly believing that he could do so without being understood by his company. Brianan may have left her in a death-trap, but this could be a lifeline at last.

"Very well." She did her best to smile at the servant and fell into step alongside them.

Fiadh slipped into Àrdish, certain that the mercenary would know the others alongside them weren't particularly learned in the southern tongue.

"Southerner, are you?" she said, finding genuine cause to smile as the mercenary desperately attempted to hide his jump of surprise.

"Aye, whit's it tae ye?" he spoke low, eyes flickering to the two servants with more suspicion they would understand than she had.

"What's your name?"

"Annis." His eyes narrowed. "Whit's yers?"

"Fiadh." The servants were paying them no mind as they continued down the hallway. No doubt they had experienced more than their share of mercenaries swapping chat in their variety of tongues and had long since learned to tune it out.

"You don't speak Cànan?" she said.

"Yer tongue? Yin wurd here an' there. Ah git by in Àrdish an' whit Sjøtunge ah picked up oan Vestamr's ships. Ah dinnae need tae ken whit yer laird says tae ken whit he wants. He's no a complicatit' man. Bide here; awa' there."

They walked in silence for a moment as Fiadh considered how directly she could phrase her request.

"How much do they pay you for your service?" she asked.

He hid his reaction well this time, eyes flitting to the servants leading them down the hall, a good sign. "Whit's it maitter tae ye?"

"I'll triple it, for one night of work."

If the mercenary had not prepared himself for a shock, he might well have shown it at that, but the most Fiadh got in return was a couple of more regular blinks and the slight crinkling of one eye in thought.

"Yin nicht? Whit fur?" His acting wasn't convincing, the suspicion and temptation both clear in his hesitant tone.

"Because if you don't say yes, I'm going to die, and I would very much like to stay on this forsaken spiral for at least a few more turns. I've got good reason to give you what I've got." Fiadh did her best to meet his eyes as they continued to walk side by side. "So, what will it be? Triple your wages for just one night and maybe learn a thing or two about the workings of a Crow?"

"If ye huv tae die, whit wid ah be daein' followin' ye there?"

He wasn't wrong. There wasn't much use in a bag full of coin if the closest you ever got to it was dangling from the belt of the man holding you under in the drowning pools.

She had to word this carefully. "There's a spirit hanging over this place, you must have felt it." He nodded, a good start. "It's not going to leave unless I rid this hall of it tonight."

"If ye dinnae?" he replied, turning the words over in his mouth.

"You all die. It has the name of every soul on this isle on its lips."

His eyebrows practically hit the ceiling in the most dramatic expression he had pulled so far. The servants took a sharp turn ahead of them and they turned into a dead-end with a single door. It was time for a decision.

"The laird haes nichtmares. He tosses an' turns in his sleep, ye think this spirit is behind thaim?" They came to the door but Annis raised a hand to quiet the servants as they turned towards them.

"I do," Fiadh replied, looking the mercenary dead in the eyes

"Ye ken how tae stop the mares?"

"Sometimes," she said. "If there's a spirit behind them."

He frowned thoughtfully. "Guid tae ken."

Annis turned to the two servants, who were looking somewhat put out from being held waiting at his hand whilst the pair spoke in a language they didn't understand. He rattled off a couple of sentences in Sjøtunge and they deliberated a moment.

Finally, the servants nodded reluctantly and moved past them and back where they had come.

Annis watched them depart before turning the latch on the door, letting it swing open, and gesturing for her to enter.

"Ah'm tae stay wi' ye, mak sure ye dinnae git up tae ony funny business while yer in the laird's hame. While ah'm 'ere ah micht as weel mak sure yer no' disturbed," he said. His expressions were unreadable, a wall of stern features and implacable deep blue eyes.

Fiadh nodded. She didn't need to know his exact reasons behind having her back right now, only that she had bought herself some brief reprieve, one that Brianan had not offered. She turned and entered the room, Annis followed and closed the door behind them.

Fiadh slumped roughly onto the cot that made up much of the sparse adornment of the chamber, dumping her sack, adjusting the scabbard swung over her back, and pinching her nose hard in thought. She had won some time, at least, but it would be useless unless she could lift the shadow hanging over Eònan before he sent his champions to finish the job that began at Tur Eumor.

"Are ye a Völva?" Annis broke her thoughts and she looked up to see him standing awkwardly in the middle of the room, arms folded and looking down on her.

"The Sjøfolk might call me that, yes," she said. "But no, I do not practice the Seidr as they do. It is a talent I have not come to master."

"Ye ken Jarl Sigurd treats his Völva weel, treats thaim like his ain wives, jist aboot."

"Hah, I bet he does. After this I might even consider his attention." There was absolutely no chance that Fiadh would ever give Sigurd the opportunity to give her such attention. She'd heard other tales about how his court treated foreign magics.

She sighed heavily. Her time was growing shorter by

the moment and dusk was approaching, bringing with it the thin sliver of an opportunity to fend off her fate.

Rising from the cot she began to unload her pack, arranging its contents in careful rows, ignoring Annis's curious eyes inspecting her work. Here went her brace of knives, there her rolls of parchment, a sack of dried foodstuffs from the voyage and her water flask.

In the centre came what would be vital for the hours ahead. Chalk, a small spherical metal device, and a roll of ancient woven cloth.

"Whit's that?"

"Nothing you need to know about," Fiadh replied, leafing through the parchments and lifting one, unfurling it and setting it out on the floor next to her. It was covered from top to base in scrawling and diagrams – her scrawling, dozens of notes she'd made over the years.

She had dedicated so much to this, searching far and wide across Seann Àite for the keys to this puzzle, for what knowledge existed about the door it unlocked. Now, for the first time, she had reached a point where there might be no other option than to discover what lay behind it.

She looked to her new companion.

"I need you to do me one more favour, even if your companions don't come for me tonight," she said.

Annis twitched an eyebrow in her direction in what appeared to be his form of an acknowledgement.

"If I do not return by the morning, the way back will be closed. I will not be coming back. Should that happen, burn the veil and destroy the orb. Should they be left intact, other things may return with the rising of the sun, things that neither you nor anyone else in these halls is capable of facing."

"Haud off till dawn, burn the cloth, break yon orb. Ah've hud harder jobs. How are ye gan tae git oot o' here?" he said.

Fiadh lifted the rolled cloth and unfurled it into the tattered veil she had found so long ago. Turning, she walked across the room and carefully laid it down in the centre of the floor.

"Through that," she declared, pointing down at it.

Annis looked at her as if she had brazenly told him that her mother was, in fact, a fish.

Fiadh shrugged and continued with her tasks, first removing her leathers and boots, leaving herself in just her sleeveless tunic, leggings, and the scabbard of Caerdrich across her shoulders. She stretched her arms out wide and enjoyed the feel of the stone flooring underneath her bare toes.

"Yer leavin' yersel' affa bare fur a rammy, Craw," he said.

"Where I'm going, I'm not going to need them. For now, I just need some air."

She set about across the room, returning to her parchments from time to time and using the chalk to mark out points and then draw the circles that ran between them. Along each line she began to chalk out the text she had detailed along the sides of the parchment, Cànan script from long before her time.

She had written these lines often enough, they were etched into her memory, but she still returned to check them over and over again, ensuring that every line was correct, every mark exactly where it should be. As she finished, she stepped back and took a spot facing across the chalk and through the window beyond at the slowly dimming sky.

Annis had stood silent through it all, his back to the door, watching the entire procedure with careful bemusement. But he had stayed, that was something, and should at least lend some hope that he would stay till the morning.

"Whit noo?" he asked as she pulled Caerdrich from across her back and laid the scabbard in her lap, the brief chill dancing across her fingertips a reminder that this was as far as the blade would tolerate being moved away from her.

"We wait until the sun touches the horizon. Then the way will be open to me, for a time, and every minute will count before I can find my way back. Till I am done that door must not be opened, these markings must not be disturbed. If I do not return, it must be destroyed."

"So be it," he replied.

"Aye," she said with a sigh. "So be it."

***

The time passed slowly. Annis stood with more calm and patience than Fiadh felt as she sat facing the window and watched the sky shift from blue to violet. Caerdrich grew cold as the time approached where she would be able to reach across to the world of the caoineag to put the spirit to rest.

Or destroy it.

With time her scratches in chalk began to shift and glow with the dull orange of the setting sun. It was working, for now at least. She looked up to see Annis's eyes fixed upon her, staring as the silver of her eyes began to shine with the coming of the dusk. He was not the first to stare, nor, she hoped, would he be the last.

When the time came the chill of the blade became a sharp stab of frost, gripping her thighs and fingertips. Fiadh stood, grasping the metal orb from the bed where she had set it aside and approached Annis.

"Your hand, please," she said as he looked at the delicately carved sphere. He held out a palm and she placed the orb upon it. With a sharp twist the intricate mechanisms shifted and Annis jerked his hand back with a hiss of pain, his blood running from a nick from the thin notched blade that extruded from its surface.

"Sorry, my own blood wouldn't do," she said, as if those words sufficed as an explanation.

Without checking to see if Annis had need for any further comment, Fiadh returned to the chalk etchings, reaching across so as not to disturb them and twisting the orb yet again at the midpoint between them, directly above the veil laid down in the floor's centre.

It clicked and a small needle emerged from its opposite side. A drop of blood fell from its tip, holding briefly before detaching from the instrument and hanging in the air, suspended by nothing.

As Fiadh stepped back across the chalk's threshold the droplet began to distort and expand, flattening into a thin translucent sheet and stretching to stand as tall as she, the remnants of the sky's light casting through it to bathe her in a crimson glow.

Caerdrich froze, the air around the blade shimmering with ice shards as the water of the air was dragged from it. Fiadh's fingers went blue around the scabbard as she gripped it tighter, the pain of the cold stabbing up her forearm.

Annis was transfixed, eyes wide, hand on the hilt of

his own blade, his back against the room's door as far from the chalk as his feet could take him.

Fiadh gave him one last look through the bright gleam of her eyes. "Hold the door, Annis," she said. "Hold it fast like your very life depends upon it."

She turned back, fixed her stance, and leapt into the blood-forged portal.

The darkness was immediate and shocking. One moment she was bathed in the twilight's glow, the next surrounded by a vast expanse of nothing. Even her feet seemed to be set on nothing in the pitch darkness, though she felt as though she was standing on the same stone tiles of the room she had left.

Fiadh looked down to discover that it was not only the room that had disappeared. She was bare as the day she was born and formless, an approximation of a human figure made of her eyes' shimmering silver.

Caerdrich still lay in her palm, the blade shining bright and unsheathed like the sun's glare off fresh snow. Gone was the cold, replaced by the strange feeling that she was suspended in nothing at all, as if the very air had been pulled away.

As the seconds passed, slowly but surely, her silvered eyes began to decipher shapes about her. There was the cot where she had left her sack, the window looking out onto yet more darkness, and Annis holding himself upright against the door, fright filling his eyes as he looked directly past where Fiadh stood.

Caerdrich did not light her path, their glow seeming only to fall upon own shifting figure.

There was no time to waste. Now that she had her bearings it was time to bring an end to this curse that had fallen upon Ghav Rhien.

She did not need to move Annis aside or pull open the door beyond; instead, she moved through it without resistance. It danced as she passed, as if it were cast in the form of a waterfall of light that her passing disturbed and splashed its shining substance across the hallway beyond.

She moved through the corridors like dust carried in a draught, sweeping past those inhabitants still gracing the halls. She could see the servants sharing hushed whispers at the passageway beyond, the priest of Alwealda gathered at the entrance to the hall with a handful of mercenaries bearing a broad collection of sharp and cruel weapons, each held at hand, but not yet drawn. They would be soon enough.

In the hall itself she heard the keening return, no longer the wavering whispers and mutters of a cry from the beyond, but words as clear as if they were being spoken into her very ear.

"Dearest Caoimhe, Domhnall, Rhona, Fionn,
the dead who lie but walk anew,
the fallen who rested now let me in,
to watch over the guilty few."

Fiadh had had enough ghostly riddles for a lifetime and wasn't about to start deciphering one now with her time drawing so perilously short. The keening continued even as she drifted through the hall and towards the Rìgh's chambers beyond, the words repeating again and again in her ear, clawing at her for attention.

The way to the Rìgh was barred by two of his champions, both looking uneasy, turning their eyes to one another and to the doorway at the sounds coming from within. She could hear Eònan's voice, his hoarse murmurs and shouts.

She stepped between the guards and took her final step to her destination.

The chamber beyond was decorated with the spoils of a lifetime of victories. Gold-tipped spears flanked one wall, embellished shields the other. Hanging above the rich fabrics of the bed that dominated the room was a grimacing wooden head bearing an iron helm.

But Eònan was not alone. Four shadows stood with their heads turned towards his form lying upon the bed. His eyes gazed up towards the ceiling, filled with fear and anguish.

Upon his chest a final figure crouched, seemingly formed of the very darkness of the beyond itself, its spindly limbs clutched close, claws of pitch gripping the Rìgh's temples, its head tilted forward to stare directly into his eyes.

Fiadh now knew what she faced. A mare, a Sjøfolk legend, a spirit come to prey upon the lost, drive them to madness and steal away their souls to fly the skies of winter. It had no place here in Seann Àite, beneath the eye of the Ríagan. It had not earned its right to stand among the spirits of this land and claim souls as its own.

"Eònan," she found herself calling to him. But he could not hear her, his mutters and shouts of fear and desperation being leached from the very air itself into the mare, whose back heaved with vicious laughter.

The four shadows paid her no mind, swaying as they stood, two tall and two short, like children. Caoimhe, Domhnall, Rhona, and Fionn. The lost family of the Rìgh, returned from the tombs in which they lay to haunt their kin and drive him to his own demise.

She took a step forward, letting the blade light the space between her and the spirits. What was not meant to be could be banished, driven out, and the peace it had disturbed restored. She had heard the tales, been raised on the stories of the heroes who cast back the spirits of foreign lands. Now, she could do the same.

The mare's silent laughter ended, its claws gripping tight and toes curling back from Eònan's chest. Its head began to twist upon its shoulders, revealing a fixed grin turning to her slowly, etched into its dark features like a knife had carved it out.

"You're not meant to be here," she snarled, fingers tightening about Caerdrich's hilt. The mare's head turned around and its gaze seemed to swallow the light around her, dragging at the frost-touched glow of the blade.

She raised Caerdrich, gripping their hilt in both hands, and ran in between the shadows to swing the blade forward and down upon the dark spirit. Its grin looked up a final time, its eyes boring into her, and for a moment she froze, hanging in the air, suspended with Caerdrich's blade raised overhead.

"Neither are you."

All at once the room seemed to expand away from her, a dark pit opening up beneath her and, with a final scream, Fiadh was pulled down into the dark.

***

She was in a long, stone corridor. But it wasn't the rough mismatched stonework of Ghav Rhien. Instead, it was smooth, perfectly carved granite, granite carved from the very mountain through which it led. Torches flickered in the dark and the smell of sea spray had been lost to the rough taste of charcoal in the air, the thickness of years of dust kicked up by her footsteps.

There was no mistaking the cold stones of Tur Eumor, nor the long halls of its inner sanctum. The corridors leading to…

Fiadh started as she realised her hands were empty, she pointlessly patted at her own form, as if she would find Caerdrich hidden in the folds of her shadow.

This is where she had found the blade, all those years ago. Why here? What business did the mare have in these halls?

She snarled at the darkness beyond the torches. Whatever it was, it could not have the blade. No good would come of uniting a haunting spirit with that ancient steel.

She turned away from where she had walked in her own distant past, away from the choice she had made to draw the blade from its stone confinement.

But within a few steps Fiadh realised this wasn't quite the hall from her memories. There was no turn in the stone ahead of her, just an endless series of the same nooks and sconces disappearing further into the dark. With each she passed another appeared out from the shadows.

She came to a stop, turned, and found the hall behind her remained just as close as it had been before she had begun.

Some kind of trap, a labyrinth forged in the mind of the mare, designed to lead her back to the blade. Maybe it wanted Caerdrich for itself, maybe this was some kind of trick to cause her to give up the blade for some cruel designs it could wage with that strength.

It was playing games with her. Wasting her time even as the Rìgh's men advanced on her chambers, as it continued to drain Eònan's will and lead him to desperately seek the aid of the worst parasites of the land.

She was done playing games.

Fiadh strode towards the hall. She knew what awaited her, the memory was burned into her mind. She had walked this path a thousand times herself, without the need of a mare seeking to torment her with it. She had tormented herself with the memory, and she'd be damned if any being was going to take that curse and make it their own.

The hall was exactly as she had left it, the same dust-coated stone, the same black drapes of the Sciathán Dubh hanging from the walls, the same white cloth draped over the plinth where the blade lay, the same three-faced statue of the Ríagan looking down upon it all. It did not whisper to her, not this time.

She advanced upon the dais, hand tearing away the cloth and revealing Caerdrich. No longer in their bright unsheathed form, but instead within the engraved black scabbard she carried upon her shoulders to this day. It all came back to this, to this moment where she had heard the blade whisper to her in the dark, guiding a desperate girl to its chamber, promised her deliverance even as invaders tore through the great fortress' grounds and hunted for the acolytes within. Where the Crows might well have turned the course of battle wielding the most powerful weapon held deep within their halls. Instead she had taken it, turned from her flight by their whispers, and they had promised her vengeance.

Caerdrich had kept her alive ever since, and it would

aid her again to free her from the mare's grasp. She reached forwards, wrapped her hand around its scabbard, and tore it free of the plinth.

The world seemed to tilt on its axis. Suddenly the plinth was above her, the corridors formerly behind her now beneath her. Fiadh hurtled down the drop, her stomach thrown into her throat with such force she didn't even have a chance to scream. With Caerdrich in one hand, she scrambled to find some, any, kind of purchase as the torch lights flew past, their flames now blazing up in the direction of the Ríagan's hall.

But now the corridor opened below to moonlight, the sounds of battle raging beyond as the mountain's stone gave way to the wide grounds beyond the walls of Tur Eumor.

Fiadh tumbled and slid across the dirt and grit, her feet desperately kicking out to gain some purchase. Her free hand dragged clear of every crack and rock as if she were falling straight down instead of along the ground.

The torches flashed in the night, lighting the silhouettes of figures engaged in a desperate fight to survive, blades held aloft, spears flying through the night. The screams of people left defenceless as blades crashed down upon them and the crack of lightning rending the stones of the walls that protected them piercing the air.

Still she spun across the ground, past the courtyard, directly towards the cliff overlooking the tumultuous waves. Her scream echoed out into the nothing and for a moment she hung in the air over the vicious crags of rock far below.

Her hand found something to grasp hold of, the loose dirt holding a root in place against the side of the cliff giving way and leaving her hanging by one arm, her torn and bloodied fingers wrapped tight around that lone root.

Hanging above the raging waters, just as she had all those years ago, tossed aside by the sorceries of those who had carved open the walls with the fury of the skies. Just as she had done a hundred thousand times in her mind, running through that moment and all the ways she could have done things differently. All the ways she could have been stronger, been able to haul herself back onto the edge and carry Caerdrich back into the fray. All the ways she could have held on for just a few more moments and been lifted free by her sisters who would surely have seen the bright blade shining in the dark.

But she was stronger now; she wasn't swallowed by the blind panic of a child facing this fall for the first time. She had been here before, and she knew how to beat it.

She flung the blade up and over the top, swinging her other hand up to the root to steady herself. Her feet found purchase on the rock, and she took a deep breath to steady her heart before the heave over the edge.

There was another crack, a flash of blinding light as another bolt struck from the heavens and cleaved through soil and rock. Caerdrich tumbled into the hollow and her breath was pounded from her lungs as the ground lurched and swung her away only to crash back into the sheer cliff face.

Fiadh could feel the panic growing again, her heart thundering against her ribs, her eyes spinning back and forth trying to spot any sign of escape through the bright spots left by the strike. Her arms grew cold and her fingers numb as blood fled her limbs and face.

There had to be a way up, this time, there had to! She

had done this before, in her thoughts, beneath every sky on the long road, in her dreams beneath every star. Her hands started to claw at the rock, but every handhold fell away at her touch, every surface turning slick as if coated with rain.

So, the rain came, torrents of it, slamming down and drowning the din of battle with the roar of thunder above.

This is not what happened. This is not what should have happened. None of it was right.

What's done is done.

Brianan's words came back to her unbidden. They rang around her head even through her desperate, gasping breaths, past the pain of her hands slipping every moment down that lone root.

What's done is done.

She hadn't clambered back up. She hadn't thought to throw the blade, even if Caerdrich had let her. She hadn't found a foothold. She hadn't been there as the last defenders of Tur Eumor fell, leaving only a ruin in their wake. Leaving no one to watch the sea when the mare came to the isle of Ghav Rhien.

She had fallen, blade in hand, robbing the citadel that had shielded and taught her of its most potent defence. She had been swallowed by the freezing waters and never again returned to the charred shell nor seen the remnants of its keepers and those ancient halls.

Fiadh had dreamt every possible way she might have saved the Tur, every far-fetched strategy a child could have drawn on to charge into battle against an army that wielded the very sky itself as a weapon.

Then, like now, Brianan's wisdom had aided her to lift herself from the dark delusions and denials of loss.

Caerdrich was in her hand once more, sliding across the rock into her waiting palm. She closed her eyes, took a final breath, and released her grip.

The wind thundered around her as she fell, the surface of the water striking her back like a hammer, before swallowing her and dragging her beneath the waves. She opened her eyes and saw only the roiling waters lit by the blade's ghostly glow.

Caerdrich began to freeze, spindles of ice snaking out, tearing loose only to reform anew in an expanding web of frost. Fiadh kicked desperately towards the surface, hand clawing skyward even as the cold began to seize her.

She broke the surface, sucked in a gulp of air, and the waters parted around her, rushing away into the darkness, and leaving her standing alone in the dark, the light of Caerdrich lighting nothing but emptiness.

Gradually the world began to form around her as ghostly shadows found their substance. The bark of great trees began to solidify around her, the darkness making way for the green of their foliage and the grass at her feet.

Where was she now? What other mazes did the mare intend to lead her down?

Fiadh wrapped her free arm around herself, shivering against the chill that still gripped her from that frozen sea. The memory of the ice was etched into her mind closer than it had been for years, the cold feeling as real as if Caerdrich's frost still wrapped about her.

There was no respite here. Flakes of snow were beginning to spiral down from between the leaves above, the grass shimmering with frozen dew.

The vegetation was verdant, too alive for such cold.

It was if the cold had been pulled with her from those icy depths, or that this was no forest of her world at all.

No moon or stars shone here to illuminate the forest beyond, no night's light to brighten her silvered eyes. She held the blade aloft and, lit by its cool glow, began to walk forward through the brush.

There was the crunch of feet on twigs ahead and Fiadh ducked behind an oak, hiding the blade's light between herself and the bark. She craned her head around the corner. This was no memory. Never before had she hidden among the boughs of some other worldly forest gripped by an unnatural winter.

Ahead, down a slope and moving with youthful abandon, was a girl. Hair as black as pitch and pale arms poking out from beneath roughly hewn hides. She moved with confidence as if her eyes, like Fiadh's own, could pierce the dark.

Behind her, stalking on the far side of the trees, was a figure with skin as white as starlight. In their hands they held a wicked two-handed blade as long again as their bare torso. From their head fell hair in a brilliant silver, and their ears protruded from beneath it in long points.

Fiadh moved in parallel to them, mirroring its movements as they followed either side of the girl in the glen.

She tracked them for a while, hand bearing the blade held low to hide its shine from the clearing, trying to see what she could do from where she was. She was too far off to ambush the pale figure across from her, and to shout from here would be to distract the child whilst warning the one stalking across the way.

Why here? What could the mare want from her,

showing her this distant scene from another time and place?

Distracted by her thoughts, Fiadh wasn't paying close enough attention to where she put her feet. She froze as she heard the crunch beneath her step, eyes immediately going across to the valley floor and to the girl whose eyes were now cast up into the trees where she stood.

She hesitated only a moment before ducking behind a tree and struggling to calm her breathing. She had recognised that face, those flecks of silver in those wide dark eyes.

Orlaith, here, in this mysterious wood in a dream spun by a mare.

She leant around and looked across the gap around the other side of the tree, but the pale man was no longer there, vanished into the foliage beyond.

She could stay here, walk to Orlaith, protect her, ensure she did not come to harm.

No, she realised, she couldn't. She could have done that a long time ago. She could have remained at the Three Willows and kept watch over the child and ensured the fey kept up their side of the bargain. But she didn't. She rode away, continued with her life, for years never returning to that place.

Now the mare was tormenting her with that. Like lifting Caerdrich from their plinth in Tur Eumor, like her fall into the ocean below, she had made those choices. She could not take them back in a dream. Her heart strained, screamed at her to walk around the tree and down to take the child into her arms and apologise for having left. But it was not Orlaith. It was a dream and no matter what she did, the mare would drag her back to do it again.

There wasn't time for her heart.

So, she took a breath and, without looking back, walked away into the trees.

They faded away before her, disappearing back into the shadows even as she continued to walk through the dark.

"Where are you?" her shout surprised even herself, seeming to echo back from walls she could not see.

"Reveal yourself! Face me, you coward! I am done with these games; I am done with you!" She slashed the air with Caerdrich, their glow leaving behind a trail of sparks.

She screamed into the dark, a wordless, formless howl of rage and grief. Tears came to her eyes as her hoarse throat gave way to sobs, broken by more screams at the nothing around her. The emotion spilled out from her, the heat of her anger ebbing away.

In the distance a light sparked to life, the orange glow of flame gradually growing as she raised her eyes to it.

Feeling drained, but lighter for it, Fiadh approached.

A lone fallen trunk barred the way towards the light and upon it sat a figure, sitting away from her, the fire's light extending out beyond him as though cast from his eyes.

A great fur cape sat upon his shoulders and Fiadh could see the blade in his lap, already dripping blood onto the grass at his feet. Red hair fell upon his back and over it sat an iron helm.

The same helm that hung in the chambers of Eònan in the halls of Ghav Rhien.

The scene shifted. Shadows of the Rìgh stood from where he sat and moved into the home beyond, with hands raised. She saw one shadow stabbing the blade into the ground and walking away, another shouting into the home's empty doorway, one drawing blood from his own hand and displaying it into the night. The last fell upon his own blade.

Through it all, Eònan sat on that fallen bough, watching in silence.

The flames beyond crackled and popped. From time to time she saw shadows grappling on the edges of the light, blades rising and falling, the echoes of screams from voices long forgotten.

Whispers hung in the air, crowding the space between her and the Rìgh, beckoning and tempting him to lift his blade and advance into the house to claim what he was owed, protect his people, be the leader that they deserve. In this memory, in this far away time of Eònan's past, he too had heard those whispers coming to him from the dark.

Fiadh advanced cautiously, but as she raised her blade to light her path, she found that Caerdrich was once again in their scabbard, that she was clothed in hardened leathers and her tough boots crumpled the ground at her feet. The symbol of the stag riding a wave adorned her chest. In this place she had become one of Ghav Rhien's own guards, another of the figments of Eònan's own dream.

With care she advanced, sliding into the edge of Eònan's vision, and as he remained still, she came to sit beside him and gaze at the flames lapping against the walls before him.

They sat in silence for a moment, Eònan's eyes fixed on the blood-stained hands wrapped around his blade, Fiadh's own on the fires leaping up the walls and thatch, neither giving warmth nor burning away the wood.

"You were not here, were you?" the Rìgh finally said. "I recognise your face, but not from this place. Not from this night."

He looked up and she saw shock register beneath the anguish, his eyes going wide as they saw the silver gazing back.

"The Crow? Here? Even in my dreams." His hands twisted tighter around his blade, blood pooling between his fingers, but he did not raise it. "It is true I sent my men to bring an end to you, finally, but foul magics have brought your spirit to me even from beyond the grave, to bring vengeance for your death at my hand."

The shock twisted and faded, giving way to sorrow.

"What poetry it is that vengeance would come to me here, before the display of my reign's cruellest act, to wash away the blood that has stained me so with my own."

"I'm not here to kill you, Eònan, though perhaps it is what you deserve. Nor have I come to offer you some kind of deliverance," Fiadh broke her silence, the firelight dancing in her eyes. "I think it is past time that you left this place behind, don't you?"

"I can't," he replied.

Fiadh turned to see he had raised his head and was now staring directly ahead, into that dark doorway directly ahead, past the dancing fires and battling shadows.

"I've tried everything," he said. "I've walked away, I've taken my own life, I've run into the fires myself and burned as I attempted to free them. Nothing I have done is enough, nothing can remove the stain of what I have done."

The whispers continued to swirl about them, coming close, feeding temptations and coercions into their ears. They promised fame and riches, they threatened death and being lost, forgotten, to the sea.

"They were my kin. Vestamr came and with his coming came their deaths. I saved Ghav Rhien from destruction. They paid with their lives for our isle's future."

"You killed them," Fiadh said.

He turned to look at her and met her eyes with those words. Beneath his helm it was not the eyes of the Rìgh of Ghav Rhien that looked back, but the black pits of the mare.

"I had no choice," he said, his voice contorted and strained, like it was being pulled from a place far away.

Fiadh cast her arm out at the scene that his memories had cast before them. "Yet you have spent all this time showing what other decisions you could have made. Each time you are returned here to start anew and make a new choice, and each time you do not make the choice you made then. You had a choice."

Those foreign eyes turned back to the flames and it dawned on Fiadh what had occurred here, why it was that the caoineag wailed day after day in the halls of Ghav Rhien, slowly driving the Rìgh and his house to madness. Caoimhe, Domhnall, Rhona, and Fionn. They weren't dead, not to him. They continued to haunt his mind even as the years passed. The mare had found that guilt and denial and made it real in this place, where the dead could live again and plague the mind of Eònan. They had been dragged from the grave to live again and haunt this man, and as long as he held them here, unable to accept the path he had chosen, they remained trapped at the border between life and death.

The caoineag cried for them, not for Eònan. It cried for their release from this dark place.

"What's done is done," she spoke Brianan's words once more, as if they were her own. "You cannot deny the past, nor can you change it. You used this blade and you wrought death with it. That cannot be changed."

"Then why am I here?" he asked. "If not to change what I have done, why return me to this place?"

Fiadh shrugged.

"Why are either of us here? You tried to have me killed, and when I tried to drive the mare from your chambers, I was dragged through the moments which my mind has clung to most. Perhaps the twisted intent of the mare is to trap us here using our drive to change what cannot be changed."

She turned to him and met that empty, haunted gaze with her own. "Why did you seek to have me killed? Why now, and why then? Why did you burn Tur Eumor?"

Eònan hesitated, his body stiffening at the question.

"It may not have been long after the return of Vestamr," he said. "But it was not my past I wished to change at Tur Eumor, it was my future. I spoke with the Norns in the hope of freedom from what I had done, and they gave me no answers. They did, however, foretell that one day a Crow would come to me and bring with them the finality of death. When the Raven came to me with her designs to destroy the halls of the Ríagan, I could finally be assured no Crow would ever bring about my end."

"The Raven indeed came to my hall, and with the Norns' prophecy fresh in my mind, I promised her my ships with which to besiege the Tur. I watched the sky fall upon it across the sea and have never felt such dread, but with it I felt a release from that curse. It fell, and with it I felt like I had saved myself. Yet here you are."

"So, I am here to deliver the finality of death," Fiadh replied, standing from where she had sat at his side.

"Perhaps, yes, my time has come. Fitting that it might be my own actions that would lead to my death. I was not owed my freedom from it. I could not free myself of the curse of blood shed by drowning it in more blood, after all. I should have known that." Eònan did not meet her eyes once more, instead staring into the sky beyond, as if preparing to see nothing at all. Opening his hands, he allowed his sword to tumble to the ground.

"That would be too easy," she said at last, releasing her hands from the hilt of Caerdrich.

He started at that and brought his gaze back to her, his eyebrows displaying a surprise that those black pits could not.

"You are not here so you might be struck down in some kind of twisted penance for your actions. I am not here to deliver that to you as a reward for the lives you cut short, for the life I may never have due to your choices. You are here to face what you have done and accept it, finally, after so many years making excuses and denials."

Once she had begun, she felt unable to stop. "You butchered your own kin because of the threat they posed to your continued prosperity on this isle. You helped the Raven burn the house of a God because another threat had dared to be raised to your rule. You do not deserve salvation."

Fiadh kicked his sword back to his feet from where

it had fallen.

"Lift your blade, accept the choice you made and make it anew. Maybe then you will be freed of this spirit and have a chance to earn your forgiveness. The mare may be gone when you wake, but your guilt has not gone, and you will have to live with that till the end of your days. You may never atone for the death you have wrought."

Eònan's mouth opened and closed like words should have emerged but he simply had not thought to create them. He looked down at the blade, his hands clenching and releasing in his lap. With a final pause, he gripped its handle to pull it from the grass, pulled his shoulders back, and stood.

"If this works," he said, eyes fixed on the burning thatch. "If I am freed of this spirit, what can I offer you in return?"

"Ideally, I should like to live on this earth a little longer," she replied. "One day, I may speak your name and ask something else of you, and you must answer my call then. I place this geas upon you, Eònan, may you never know the consequences of breaking it."

Eònan nodded, and, with a final look in her direction, walked into the flames.

Where he had waited a small creature sat, black as pitch, spindly limbs curled up underneath it. A fixed, jagged grin turned to meet her. It looked at her for a time, those twisted features revealing nothing of its intent. Then, finally, it lifted one arm in a wave. The mare faded and with it the flames, shadows, and Eònan himself vanished from view.

In the darkness, for a moment, Fiadh felt a sense of peace. The pressure on her chest was lifted, the burn in her throat from her screams had eased. For that blissful moment, her thoughts were empty of the whispers that had trailed her for so long.

Then she felt the scabbard of Caerdrich become chill once more and, with a curse, she began to fall.

***

When she blinked open her eyes the whole world was crimson. She was back in her chambers in Ghav Rhien, dawn's glow shining light onto the ceiling.

She was... wet. Slick from head to toe. With her free hand she wiped her eyes free and looked down to see she was coated in slick, bright, blood. Horrified, Fiadh turned back to the window and found that the gateway she had opened before had collapsed with her return, splashing across the floor.

There was a clatter from the doorway, and she turned to find Annis standing absolutely still, eyes fixed upon her, from the other side of the frame.

Only the frame. The door itself was split into pieces, some lying across the floor and some hanging from the remaining hinges. One body lay inside the room, moving very slowly and groaning from time to time, barely inches from the chalk that surrounded her. Another lay underneath Annis' feet in the doorway itself, the blood trail showing they had been thrown face-first into the door's frame.

Annis stood with the same look of frozen shock that he had had when she first opened the portal. One torn-off leg of the cot that had previously held her belongings had fallen from his fingers, the cot itself now shredded and impaled by one end of a spear shaft.

He was not alone. Beyond the door stood two more of his colleagues, between them the priest of Alwealda, hand clutching his face, blood running between his fingers where half of his mask had once been.

The group had halted mid-motion, blades raised, one bearing a shield still holding Annis' axe and barring his path.

Fiadh twisted her face into a snarl, gnashing her teeth and raising Caerdrich, held again within their scabbard, towards them.

"Begone, priest," she said, dropping her voice into a growl. "Run from this place as swiftly as they can carry you, before I seize your soul and drag it down into the pit with me!"

The silence was broken only by the sound of blood dripping from her clenched fist. But that was enough. Still holding his shattered mask close the priest fled, almost tripping over his vestments as he vanished up the corridor, swiftly followed by the remnants of his companions.

Annis watched them go, a look of bemusement replacing his shock as he turned back to her, hands raised in question.

"Thanks," Fiadh said, trying to wipe her hand free of the blood she had uselessly smeared across her face.

"Yer welcome," came Annis' reply, as he lifted one half of a white marble mask in his other hand and gave her the first smile she had seen from him.

In spite of herself, Fiadh laughed.

***

The waves lapped at the shore, washing back and

forth over the pebbles beneath the docks. Fiadh stood looking over the sea, enjoying the breath of fresh air running over her skin.

The ship was ready, her pack loaded and the crew gradually shifting the last of their cargo of fish and wood carvings from the jetty.

Brianan stood with her, as he had done for some time, looking in silence over the water. It does the mind good, he had always said, to take some time to drink in the world around you without feeling the need to break it.

That might be true, Fiadh thought, but she did have a question.

"Brianan?" she asked.

"Yes?"

"There's one thing beyond the veil, something Eònan said that I can't shake from my mind," she said.

"The dreams of another are a dangerous place, Fiadh. Be careful what you bring back with you." His voice was as stern as ever. The shadow may have been lifted from Ghav Rhien, the caoineag laid to rest alongside the spirits it had cried for, but the druid forever spoke as though he carried the world upon his shoulders.

"Eònan he... he said a Raven came to him many years ago. This Raven, they burned the Tur, or at least he said that they did. Who are they?" she asked.

She could see Brianan looking at her out of the corner of his eye, weighing his answer. He knew, possibly more than he would ever reveal to her, but even a little could guide her to where she needed to go.

"The Red Raven," he said, finally. "She goes by many names, has ruled one of these hundred isles for longer than I have lived, plying her trade as a useful ally for whomever might be in need of one on these tumultuous seas."

He sighed and joined her to watch over the water. "Given how long she has ruled, it may be that the name is more of a title than a name. I did not know she was at the Tur, but then, the stories would have it be that she has been at many places even when she could not have been."

He paused for a moment before adding, "Do not chase her, Fiadh. The Raven is not spoken of in hushed tones for her talents with generosity and good will. If she were indeed behind the burning of the Tur, it would be a gift to bring her the one acolyte of the Ríagan who got away."

Fiadh played at a thoughtful frown. "Maybe then I must bring her an even greater gift, some trinket she might have seen that is more within the reach of a crow than a raven. Aren't we infamous for picking up the shiny scraps left by those long departed?"

Brianan laughed at that, and it was a warm, chesty chuckle that brought a genuine smile to her lips.

"There isn't anything that might change your course when you have one, is there? I see my work here is done. You have my thanks." He turned to her and offered a hand. "You may not know it but what you did here matters more than you could believe. So many will rest easier tonight. Not just the Rìgh sequestered in his chambers."

She took his hand and they shook, pausing a moment to exchange smiles they had not shared for many years. With a final nod, Brianan gave her shoulder a squeeze and walked away back towards the fortress above.

Fiadh returned to her place, letting out a sigh of

breath she had been holding for far too long, looking out at the sails dancing on the distant waves.

She heard the footsteps coming from behind her but did not turn, raising her gaze only to fix on the mountains of Seann Àite beyond.

"Ye huvnae left?"

Annis stood alongside her, taking the place the druid had left. He crossed his arms as he cocked his head, staring off into the distance trying to spot whatever she could be looking at.

"Not yet. It's a lovely day, figured I might as well enjoy it for a while," she said.

"Aye, 'tis that. It'll be a guid day fur a journey."

She paused for a moment, considering how to phrase her question for him for the second time in as many days.

"Do you want to come with me?" she said, keeping her tone light. "I could use someone like you watching my back. How many did you turn back at that door, four? Five? I may need that distraction again one day, maybe a few more times."

There came that matter-of-fact shrug again. "Are ye guid at whit ye dae?" he said, with an eyebrow raised sceptically.

"If I weren't, I wouldn't be offering to share half of what I get. If I'm not, you can feel free to find someone else who can offer you more coin," Fiadh said, turning to look at him.

Annis' eyes drifted to the pair of sacks lying in the bow of the ship alongside her and then to her eyes. "Ye kent ah'd say aye."

Fiadh's smile broke wider at that. He had taken long enough. "I knew that troupe of misfits wasn't giving you the escape you needed. You're too curious to turn away from a chance to know what happened in that room. I know you don't want to go back to standing beside the throne of a sad old man again."

She tossed the bag Eònan's men had delivered in his stead in one hand, peering thoughtfully at it before tossing it over to her companion. Annis caught it without breaking her gaze.

"I know you're wondering if there's more gold where that came from," Fiadh said. "There will be. So yes, I knew you'd say yes."

A thoughtful frown and nod came with that. Then, without a further word, he turned and jumped into the waiting ship.

"So," he said, eyes on her again. "Whaur's next?"

ABOUT THE AUTHOR

Tristan Gray was a latecomer to Scotland, moving to the north from Jersey in 2014.

After years of searching to find the real spark behind his writing Scotland unlocked it - The rugged country and dark history, which also inspired the works of George R. Martin and Diana Gabaldon, gave new meaning to the fantasy tales of his childhood.

Now, with a new connection to an adopted home driving his work, and inspiration stretching from conventional novels, to graphic novels, to games, Tristan is writing tales worthy of the inspiration by the land around him.

He can be found at his website:
tristangraywrites.com

Printed in Great Britain
by Amazon